Anonymous

# Symptoms and Treatment of Malignant Diarrhoea

Anatiposi

**Anonymous**

# Symptoms and Treatment of Malignant Diarrhoea

Reprint of the original.

1st Edition 2023 | ISBN: 978-3-38210-282-1

Anatiposi Verlag is an imprint of Outlook Verlagsgesellschaft mbH.

Verlag (Publisher): Outlook Verlag GmbH, Zeilweg 44, 60439 Frankfurt, Deutschland
Vertretungsberechtigt (Authorized to represent): E. Roepke, Zeilweg 44, 60439 Frankfurt, Deutschland
Druck (Print): Books on Demand GmbH, In de Tarpen 42, 22848 Norderstedt, Deutschland

# SYMPTOMS AND TREATMENT

OF

# MALIGNANT DIARRHŒA;

BETTER KNOWN BY THE NAME OF

# ASIATIC CHOLERA,

AS TREATED IN THE ROYAL FREE HOSPITAL

*During the Years* 1832, 1833, 1834, 1848, & 1854.

BY

LONDON:

WYMAN & SONS, GREAT QUEEN STREET,

LINCOLN'S INN FIELDS, W.C.

1871.

# DEDICATION TO THE FIRST EDITION,
## 1834.

---

### TO HIS ROYAL HIGHNESS
# THE DUKE OF GLOUCESTER.

---

SIR,

Having for seven years been the senior
surgeon of that excellent Institution, the
Free Hospital, over which your Royal
Highness presides, I trust that no apology
is required for making known the result of
my observations on the Nature, or Treatment, of any of those Malignant Diseases
which that Institution was more especially
designed to treat ; and less so, with reference to that destructive pest, known by the
name of Malignant Cholera.

In publishing that knowledge, which has

B

been acquired by a careful, laborious, and long attendance on the sufferers, I am influenced only by a desire to be instrumental in establishing a mode of treatment by which the destructive career of the disease may be arrested.

In dedicating this small work to your Royal Highness, it is in the hope, from its being the first attempt at a practical arrangement of the symptoms and treatment of a new malady, that the imperfections may be lightly viewed, and the merit, if any, meet with the approbation of your Royal Highness.

I have the honour to be,

Your Royal Highness's

Most obedient Servant,

WILLIAM MARSDEN.

2, THAVIES INN,
*September*, 1834.

# SECOND EDITION.

— ⋅◦⋅ —

To the Rev. EDWARD RICE, D.D., *Chairman,*
*and the Committee of Management of*
*the Royal Free Hospital.*

REV. SIR AND GENTLEMEN,

As it is through your exertions and
benevolence in maintaining the Royal Free
Hospital, where so many wretched fellow-
beings daily seek relief and succour, so it
is by the enormous number of extreme
cases of disease that have come under my
notice, that I am enabled to arrive at just
practical conclusions in the treatment of
some of the most malignant affections,
more especially that disease called Asiatic
Cholera ; a malady little understood by the
general body of Medical Practitioners.

In presenting to you the following Treatise, I must beg to remark, that it was during the years 1832, 1833, and 1834, that my deductions were drawn, when your Hospital was the *only one* in the Metropolis that freely admitted Cholera Patients,—all of whom were intrusted to my care; and although from 1834 to the present time, October, 1848, there has been an annual average of more than two thousand cases of Diarrhœa, not a single instance of Asiatic Cholera has been met with; but, should the disease have now re-visited this country, as it is thought to have done, and should it become generally prevalent, I feel confident that the doors of the Royal Free Hospital will be again opened, as before, to the sufferers, and I need scarcely assure you of my zealous co-operation with your other Medical Officers in meeting the danger.

Permit me to avail myself of the present opportunity of acknowledging, with gratitude, my sincere thanks to you, and to all those Philanthropic Noblemen, and Ladies and Gentlemen, who have so liberally given their support in aid of such a truly Christian Charity.

With great respect, allow me to subscribe myself,

Rev. Sir, and Gentlemen,

Your obedient Servant,

WILLIAM MARSDEN.

LINCOLN'S INN FIELDS,
*October*, 1848.

# PREFACE TO FOURTH EDITION.

REPORTS from abroad indicate that this country may again, and shortly, be visited by that terrible disease, Asiatic Cholera. Should this misfortune occur, I am afraid there is every reason to fear we shall be found little better prepared to check its ravages now than we were at former visitations. True, the sanitary condition of our towns is better; the same may be said of our Water Supply; and the Thames Shipping Inspection Committee are doing all they can, considering the difficulties with which they have to contend. Thus far we have gained, but as regards our scientific treatment of the disease I am not aware that any advance has been made. When this fearful scourge came on us, in the years 1832, 1833, and

1834, the late Dr. Marsden, ever ready to grapple with a new difficulty, at once threw open the doors of the Royal Free Hospital to all comers suffering from this disease, and the large experience he then and at subsequent periods gained, resulted in a very successful mode of treatment, the particulars of which will be found in these pages. This success has neither been superseded nor, to my knowledge, equalled : so extraordinary indeed are the records of the cases restored from collapse by the saline injection used by him, that they read more like a tale from the pages of Edgar Poe than real scenes from the wards of a London Hospital.

During the Russian War in 1854-5, when I was surgeon to the Ambulance Corps before Sevastopol, our troops suffered terribly from this disease and acute dysentery. I had then, for the first time, an opportunity of testing the efficacy of this treatment on a large scale, with a considerable amount of success. The ratio of deaths was greater than that obtained by Dr. Marsden, but the difference between the hardships at the field of war and the comfortable wards of the Royal Free Hospital will more than account for this.

In the chapter headed " Precautionary Measures," amongst other matter will be found directions as to what to eat, drink, and avoid, and I merely add the few following remarks on some sanitary points that I think of importance.

WATER.—I believe nothing is more important to health than pure water, and as far as the supply. from the Companies is concerned I do not think (with one or two exceptions) we have much reason to complain; the fault lies at home, in dirty cisterns, and I would strongly urge every one to see that these are thoroughly cleaned out, and that the same water is not allowed to remain in them too long ; it is an excellent plan to let each run out in hot weather at least twice a week, permitting the water to run freely through for a short time previous to refilling : by this means we have not only our water wholesome and fresh, but our drains kept clean and free.

AIR AND GAS.—The more fresh air the better for health : so ventilate your house freely, particularly the staircase and all rooms in which gas is burnt. Never light the gas in your bedroom till you retire for the night, or, if wanted during the evening, turn it *out* on leaving the room : nothing is more unhealthy than sleeping in a room in which gas has been burning all the evening, especially in winter time. Use some disinfectant occasionally,—I believe there is no better plan than putting a little chloride of lime on the outside ledge over the doors, and changing the same now and then.

DRAINS.—Flush the drains, sinks, water-closets, &c. (see paragraph on water), and twice a week throw down each trap and water-closet a little chloride of lime.

DUST-BIN.—This cannot be emptied too often ; and no animal or vegetable matter should be thrown there, but be burnt on the kitchen fire the last thing every night, and thus destroyed.

It would be much better, hower, if dust-bins were abolished altogether, and in place thereof, the refuse of each day should be thrown into a box or pail, these to be placed on the edge of the pavement, in front of each house, every morning, and their contents removed in carts for the purpose. This I believe is done, and answers very well, in the City.

With these remarks I introduce the work to the public, trusting my father's labours will still be found useful.

A. M.

Lincoln's-Inn Fields,
*November*, 1871.

# PRELIMINARY OBSERVATIONS.

---

IN an infectious epidemic, it is of the utmost importance to learn where and by what means it originates, the route it takes from one kingdom to another, and by what medium it is communicated from man to man; but, in an epidemy which is neither infectious nor contagious, such knowledge is of secondary consequence; and instead of employing our time in such difficult researches, it would be far better spent by endeavouring to learn the nature of the disorder and the most efficient mode of arresting the fatal consequences. This is pre-eminently the case with reference to what is called Malignant Cholera.

Gentlemen of high professional character, Dr. Barry, and others, were sent by the

British Government to St. Petersburg, and various parts of the Continent, with a view to gain information on this subject;—quarantine was established at every port;* but all was useless. The doctors returned little wiser than they went; and the disease ran over this, and almost every other country, committing its dreadful ravages alike in high or low regions,—in hot, cold, wet, or dry seasons;—baffling all human efforts to arrest its progress, or hardly even to mitigate its horrors. A Government Board of Health was established, and was continued for upwards of two years in operation; and, singular to remark, the Medical department of that Board, on the close of their labours, in the autumn of 1833, afforded the profession not the slightest knowledge on the subject, either physiological or pathological.

During the existence of the disease in

---

* Nothing can be more unnecessary than quarantine for Cholera.

1832, the directions for treatment, professional and domestic, issued by the Board, were solely founded on empirical principles; yet, notwithstanding those erroneous measures, much might have been rectified, had the Board, at the time, with every facility for so doing, proceeded to a public and impartial investigation of the nature and treatment of the malady. The disease has now paid us a third visitation; and it is saying but little for the character of our medical institutions, when I assert that up to the present time, nothing has issued to guide the profession in the treatment of such cases, either from the College of Physicians, or from the College of Surgeons.

In a country like England, it is an extraordinary fact, that with all her increased knowledge, and boasted perfection of legislation, she has no permanent watch over the health of the community; and it is only within the last few weeks of the present year, that a Board of Health has been established, but not on anything like just or sound principles.

On the first appearance of this unknown disease in London, medical men of every grade, more particularly those practising in the higher branches of the profession, on viewing the afflicted patient, became terrified and panic-struck; and the public, in consequence of their professional advisers being ignorant of the nature of this malady, were completely bewildered and paralyzed. In this state of things, and as if to produce all the consternation possible, the richly-endowed hospitals of this Metropolis closed their doors against the wretched sufferers,—the affluent inhabitants fled,—and the great and wealthy members of the faculty dared not, or would not, condescend to visit the habitations of the afflicted.

It was a scourge that fell first only upon the poor, the wretched, the dissipated, and the destitute. Of the secrets of nature, or the workings of an Almighty power, we

know but little.   We know not how soon,
or to what extent, it may become the fell
enemy of the rich and well-fed portion of
the community.   By neglecting to protect
and preserve the indigent from pestilence,
the higher grades of society lose their best
chance of preserving themselves from the
like evils.

On the appearance of the so-called
"Malignant Cholera," the Governors of
the FREE HOSPITAL, for the Cure of Malignant Diseases, in Greville Street, Hatton
Garden,* in the most prompt and effective
manner, made up fifty beds, and threw
open their doors to the indiscriminate admission of all sufferers from that disease.
In justice to the managers of that Charity,
I feel that the warmest thanks of the public
were duly merited by every member of
the Committee, not only for the care and
attention they invariably devoted to the

---

* Since removed to Gray's Inn Road, and known
as the Royal Free Hospital for the Destitute Sick.

C

comfort of the patients, but for the ample opportunities they afforded to their medical officers, for acquiring a knowledge of treating malignant and contagious diseases in general; and, more particularly, the disease in question. I have no hesitation in saying that, from the principles on which that excellent charity is conducted, the lives of thousands have been saved; and in arresting the influence of contagious disorders, its benefits are incalculable: since its foundation, in 1828, to the present time, upwards of *two hundred thousand* persons have been successfully treated, and restored from the most destructive and loathsome maladies to health and comfort. Upwards of *three hundred* patients suffering from the second stage of Cholera were admitted into the Hospital: at first, nearly every one died, although every plan of treatment that could be recommended was adopted; and it was only in despair that a mode of treatment, suggested by Dr. Stevens, was tried. Through the effects of that treatment a glimmering ray of hope was first discovered, which led to the practice now pursued, and laid down in the following paper; and on this plan alone do I believe it possible for the life of a single patient to be rescued from the second, or collapsed stage of the complaint. On the other hand, I feel equally assured that confidence and discretion in the use of calomel during the first stage will remove the disorder in ninety-nine cases out of every hundred, without the slightest future injury being sustained by a single individual from this medicine.*

During the months of July and August, 1834, twenty-six patients were admitted in the second stage, and only ten recovered; from which it would appear that more were lost than saved. Unfortunately for the sufferers, scarcely one was ever sent

---

* During the year 1848, upwards of 500 cases of severe diarrhœa have been successfully treated in the Hospital by this plan.

into the Hospital until all hope of recovery was given up by their previous medical attendants; what chance, then, but the slenderest had any plan of treatment under such circumstances? Notwithstanding this, some of the very worst cases were restored, both by the saline medicine and by the saline injection : and so confidently do I rely on the success of these remedies for combating this extraordinary disease, that we need no longer view with horror and dismay the approach of this enemy to human existence. Several important facts will be noticed in the cases given to illustrate the merit of the treatment; which, if not satisfactory to some individuals, I trust will be found sufficiently important to the philanthropic practitioner to induce and promote unprejudiced investigation.

It is a subject of the utmost importance, both to the profession and the public, to distinguish between infectious and non-infectious diseases ; and I have not, during a practice extending over a period of forty

years, met with a single instance contro-
verting the principle that I shall lay down
with reference to these points. Infectious
disorders never attack a human being a
second time; and those maladies which are
communicated from one person to another,
through the medium of the atmosphere,
such as small-pox, scarlet-fever, measles,
and hooping-cough, constitute nearly the
whole class of infectious disorders peculiar
to man. Plague, typhus-fever, malignant
cholera, and a great many other alarming
and destructive pests, which are epidemic,
but not infectious, may attack the same
persons many times. Contagious disorders
are altogether of a different class to either
of the preceding, and may, by contact only,
be communicated an indefinite number
of times.

Infectious diseases may always be retained amongst us by artificial means, at
least so long as human beings are to be
found who have not had the disorder; and
contagious maladies may exist for an un-

limited period, or be repeated an indefinite number of times in the same individual; while, on the contrary, an epidemic disease, such as Cholera, Plague, &c., cannot be retained by artificial means, nor extended beyond the range of its general influence, nor does the first attack exempt from a second. On the return of the like epidemy, it may again affect the persons who had previously suffered; hence the folly of quarantine.

Some persons may object to the division made in this paper; but it is of the utmost importance to divide the progress of the disease into two stages, in order that the treatment of the one should not be erroneous, and in direct opposition to that required for the other. After my first paper appeared making this division, in 1832, the Government Board of Health immediately issued a paper making three divisions; but for all practical and useful purposes, two will be found sufficient.

Much time has been devoted to the investigation of the blood by Drs. Clanny, O'Shaughnessy, and others; others, again, have endeavoured by every means to effect what they term the unlocking of the secretions; and some have ransacked the Pharmacopœia for the most powerful stimulants, under the impression that to restore the pulse by such means was all that was required to preserve the patient.

To investigate the character of the blood was rational, and attended with beneficial results; but in attempting to unlock the secretions, or restore the circulation by stimulants, in the advanced stage of the disease, until the volume of blood had been sufficiently restored, was only to shorten still more the life of the sufferer. Some persons relied greatly on external applications, such as mustard-poultices, blisters, camphor-liniments, &c.; while another, considered more knowing than all the rest, proposed, and absolutely practised, a mechanical mode of arresting the discharge, by plugging up the outlet of the intestines : why this learned gentleman did not close the upper aperture as well as the lower, I am at a loss to learn.

I now conclude these preliminary observations, and, with as much perspicuity and conciseness as possible, enter on my views of the nature and treatment of what is understood by the erroneous name " Cholera Morbus."—This name implies a morbid flow of bile : while in this new disease, when fully developed, there is neither bile, nor any secretion whatever from the liver. Cholera Morbus is a disease peculiar to tropical climates, occasionally occurring during the hot seasons in temperate climates, and it consists in a violent action of the liver, secreting morbid bile, accompanied by violent fever, spasm, &c. I therefore take the liberty of giving this malady the name of Malignant Diarrhœa ; for an evil very destructive in its consequences, and not yet obviated, was occasioned through the introduction of this disorder under the erroneous title of

Cholera Morbus : every professional man knew what was understood by such a name, and many how to treat such a disease; while, on the first appearance of the malady in question, in 1832, the profession was quite baffled, both as to its nature and treatment, and to this time continue nearly equally in the dark.

There can be no doubt that this disorder has exercised its ravages in tropical climates ; but for want of careful investigation it has been viewed only as a more severe form of Cholera Morbus.

# MALIGNANT DIARRHŒA;

*Better known by the incorrect name of* ASIATIC, SPASMODIC, OR MALIGNANT CHOLERA.

---

THIS is an epidemic disease, neither contagious nor infectious; that is to say, one which cannot, by artificial means, be communicated from one individual to another, but may affect the same person an unlimited number of times. The progress of the symptoms varies, from two causes: one, the extent to which a patient is affected by the poison; the other, from the powers of resistance occasioned by the good or bad constitution of the individual afflicted. Persons of the same family or living in every respect under similar circumstances, may be, and frequently are, affected simultaneously, or in succession;

and, were it not for the varied localities,
different modes of living, habits, and constitutions of the people, the whole community of any place affected would suffer
alike from this or any other epidemy. I
believe the poison occasioning this disorder is contained in the atmosphere: how
generated, is not known,—but I think it
is the atmosphere overcharged with water
and miasma,—for we are equally in the
dark respecting the origin of all epidemic
diseases. By breathing this morbific atmosphere, the blood becomes affected
through the medium of the lungs; and,
like all other poisons, it produces its specific
effect, which in this malady, is to determine that important fluid, in an extraordinary degree, to the surface of the intestines, where it deposits its thinner and
more fluid parts, called the serum or water
of the blood. Every production in nature
on which we cannot feed, must be considered, more or less, a poison: arsenic,
mercury, rhubarb, jalap, prussic acid,

ipecacuanha, &c., have their specific actions on the constitution; and the squirting cucumber produces effects approaching the disease in question so nearly, as to render it difficult to distinguish the one from the other.

The evidence of an approaching attack of malignant Cholera, consists in a sense of pain or uneasiness in the bowels, with purging, nausea, loss of appetite, thirst, and extreme prostration of strength. Now during the existence of this epidemy, all persons experience, more or less, these sensations; and I believe that all would be equally affected were it not, as before stated, for the variety of constitutional powers of resistance. The half-starved wretch, the emaciated debauchee, also the susceptible and delicate amongst the higher classes of society, are equally liable to the sudden ravages of this disease: while the healthy and well-fed possess the faculty of throwing off the poison by the ordinary functions of the excretory organs : and it is only when the action of the liver and kidneys fails in discharging this function, that the second or collapse stage supervenes. It is idle to suppose that an individual cannot be affected by this disease, unless he has got all the symptoms of collapse; and it is of the utmost importance to know that by attending to the premonitory signs, we should, in ninety-nine out of every hundred cases, prevent the second stage.*

On the presumption that in this malady the blood contains the morbific principle, the indications would naturally be to excite the action of both the liver and kidneys,—these organs being especially designed in the animal economy for the purpose of removing from that fluid all useless and adventitious matter. The

---

* At the Free Hospital, during the years 1832-33, out of five hundred patients in the first stage, only twelve ran into the second ; and eventually, only four died.

disease itself, in the first instance, more or
less irritates the liver, and sufficiently so,
in constitutions previously healthy and
robust, to carry off the offending matter;
but in delicate habits, assistance in general
is required; and it is astonishing to wit-
ness the extraordinary effects of large
doses of calomel : indeed, this medicine
cannot be administered too boldly, inas-
much as small doses produce no effect,
while a full dose acts almost like magic,
and the happiest results ensue. All in-
convenience subsides in persons whose
bowels have been incessantly relaxed from
twelve to twenty-four hours together, on
their taking from fifteen to thirty grains of
this preparation; and so completely are
the distressing symptoms allayed, that in
the short space of fifteen to twenty minutes,
no further evacuation will occur, unless an
active purgative be given, which should be
administered four hours afterwards. This
purgative must not be of a saline nature,
as it would be apt to induce a relapse of

the same diarrhœal action of the bowels as before, but one of an active vegetable kind —castor oil and tincture of rhubarb have been found the most suitable. Tincture of rhubarb produces a powerful muscular contraction of the intestine, while the oil mechanically lubricates the surface. It is rarely requisite to give a second dose of either medicine, but if otherwise they should be equally potent.

Opium, narcotics, and all stimulants of a spirituous kind, irritate, diminish, and eventually destroy the function of the liver.* Consequently they are particularly injurious in this disorder; and when given, even with calomel, seldom if ever produce the desired effect. Calomel *alone* must be relied on.

When the calomel has subdued the nausea and diarrhœa, and the purgative

---

* Drunkards and persons who had deranged the function of the liver by taking such remedies, were the first victims to this disease.

draught has been taken, stools of a black gelatinous nature, resembling half-melted pitch, will pass off; and, in the majority of cases, no further medical aid is required.

During the existence of this stage of the disease, we should rigidly enjoin abstinence from all fluids, beyond a sufficiency to moisten the mouth; for if copious draughts of barley-water, toast and water, or any other fluid, be taken, vomiting, in all probability, will continue, and preclude the possibility of either the mercury or the draught having their desired effects.

It is well to order the patient small doses of simple effervescing mixture, or soda-water, about two table-spoonfuls to be taken with the calomel, and repeated every hour, so long as the circumstances of the case require. The effervescing saline has a powerful tendency to tranquillize that irritable state of the stomach, which generally accompanies the progress of this stage of the disorder.

D

## SECOND STAGE, OR COLLAPSE.

The symptoms of which are, violent vomiting and purging, a total suspension of the action of the liver and kidneys, loss of pulse, livid extremities, clean tongue, cold breath, blueness of the lips, and intolerable thirst. These symptoms do not arise from any sedative effect produced on the brain, or nervous system ; but, from the poison exciting certain nerves,* which determine the circulation to the surface of the bowels, there occasioning a mechanical separation of serum from the blood, and diminishing the volume of that necessary fluid so seriously, as to preclude the

---

* I believe the mesenteric nerves are alone excited ; and the increased vascular action exists only in their corresponding arteries. The fluid contained in the stomach is not given solely from its own service ; but by the spasmodic contraction of the upper intestines, a considerable quantity is mechanically forced through the pylorus. It is more than probable that the pancreas is considerably engaged in secreting this fluid.

possibility of the heart propelling its contents in sufficient quantity to reach the
extremities, or to preserve the action of
the excretory or secretory organs, notwithstanding the contracted state of the vascular system. Besides, the blood is in too
viscid a state to pass the capillaries;
hence the great vital depression from the
want of due action over the surface of the
brain and nervous chords.

The function of the liver and kidneys
ceases, as before stated, not by any sedative
effect of the poison, but entirely through
the want of a due supply of blood being
transmitted to these organs; and unless
we succeed in increasing the volume, either
by natural or artificial means, we shall
most assuredly fail in restoring a single
patient. Several cases will be found in the
concluding part of this paper, fully illus-
trating this principle.

There is a considerable desire to drink,
from the commencement of this disorder,
but the extraordinary thirst does not come

on until the diarrhœa has continued for some time ; and here nature points out in a forcible manner, as she generally does, the most valuable indication of cure. Drink! drink! exclaim the poor wretches ; while at the same instant, the whole alimentary canal, from the termination of the œsophagus to that of the colon, is powerfully distended with a fluid as limpid as water, with the exception of some flocculi—this fluid is the poisoned serum of the blood, slightly decomposed.

The extent to which a patient has a desire to drink, may be formed by the following facts. In ordinary cases, during collapse, from two quarts to one gallon per hour will be taken ; but ten patients, who were restored in the Free Hospital, in 1832, drank two hundred and twenty-five gallons of water in seventy-eight hours ; and one patient, who died, took forty gallons within ninety-six hours.

Now it appears extraordinary that so intense a thirst should exist under such circumstances; but the following seems to be the cause:—That the exudation from the extremities of the arteries over the immense surface engaged in this peculiar action, far exceeds the power of the lacteals to replace in time sufficient to preserve the circulation; besides, the very fluid absorbed is of a poisonous character, and will, the moment it reaches the arterial system, continue its specific influence, and be again deposited in the intestines. This action continues until the blood has either freed itself from the morbific principle, or until the patient sinks.

What then but this can be the obvious inference, either to the scientific or empirical practitioner? Get rid of the offending fluid, and permit as little as possible to be re-absorbed and returned to the circulation. This, in a great many cases, may be accomplished by the most simple means. The moment the patient either vomits or purges, let him instantly swallow as much water as possible. It is of no use

attempting to give nutritious fluids of any
kind, as digestion is completely suspended :
let a vigorously repulsive action of the
stomach be excited ; and the best means of
so doing, is by strong and repeated doses
of saline solution.  Several important ob-
jects are gained by this mode of exhibiting
the saline: first, it instantaneously evacuates
the stomach; and secondly, by some portion of the saline solution descending
through the intestines, and mixing with
the fluids exuding from their surface, and
with the water previously taken, forms
with them a compound containing less deleterious matter, consequently better suited
to unite with the dark carbonaceous blood
that remains in the vascular system.   The
saline also stimulates the lacteals more
powerfully than any other preparation is
known to do; it is also powerfully anti-
septic, and a necessarily component part of
the blood.   These are circumstances of the
utmost importance ; for if we succeed in
exciting the vessels to take up fluid ade-

quate to preserve the circulation until the blood has parted with all its morbific properties, we shall then, and not until then, restore the patient.

It may be asked, why not give a weak saline drink in place of pure water ? The reasons for not doing so are these :—When the patient finds his stomach so distended by fluid that it is difficult to be ejected, a strong saline solution will instantaneously effect that object ; immediately after which we should give the patient pure water, it is more grateful than any other drink, and is not so readily rejected, but in a great measure passes into the intestines, diluting the deleterious character of the fluid already there. By repeating the saline dose every fifteen minutes we are sure to have some portion pass into the bowels, and, I believe, sufficient to effect the object desired ; while on the other hand, were saline drink only to be administered, however weak, an incessant vomiting would ensue, and little or no water would pass

beyond the stomach. I wish particularly
to impress on the minds of medical men
who may have such cases under their
charge, that their success in treatment
depends on the stomach and bowels being
occupied by a more healthy fluid than that
deposited in these organs through the
diseased action.

Suppose, after the administration of the
above plan, no restoration of pulse takes
place, and the patient continues rapidly to
sink, what is to be done ?   The answer is
evident; that having failed to restore the
volume of blood by the action of the lac-
teal absorbents, a vein must be opened,
and a fluid corresponding in character as
nearly as possible to the serum of the
blood, must be injected in sufficient quantity to fully restore the pulse at the wrist;
at the same time endeavouring to arrest
further exudation from the capillaries of
the intestines, by astringents carefully administered—opium and bark are the best;
and this is the only period from the begin-

ning of the disease at which the exhibition of opium or astringents are recommended. Should, however, the diarrhœa continue, the circulation will, in proportion to that action, again decline, which renders this the most important time for diligently watching your patient, many having been lost by leaving them too long unseen; for the moment the pulse begins to sink, we must again resort to the injection, and repeat it at periods, proportionate to the urgency of the case and character of the patient. In giving astringents at this time, I advise for an adult, ten drops of laudanum, with one ounce of compound tincture of bark to be taken without any dilution, every half-hour, until the diarrhœa entirely ceases.

If we succeed in sustaining the pulse for twelve hours, and the diarrhœa ceases, we may consider, the patient safe; but the utmost caution must be observed with respect to nutriment. Nothing stronger than gruel and broth must be permitted for the first two or three days; afterwards rice, or any other farinaceous puddings, with small draughts of malt liquor, for the space of four to six days; from which time the patient must be managed according to circumstances. Urine will generally be secreted, and evacuated six hours after the restoration of the pulse ; the liver will likewise begin to resume its function, throwing out for the first two days a green fluid, afterwards yellow, and lastly, healthy bile. When a patient is restored by these means, it frequently happens that after the first two days symptoms of cerebral disturbance, of a typhoid character, supervene ; which must likewise be treated according to the urgency and circumstances of the case. With ordinary care, such cases rarely prove fatal. I lost only two patients that had fully rallied by injection ; both lived about twelve days after the injection, and had a powerful pulse nearly the whole time ; I believe they died from cerebral effusion.

In giving this disease a place in medical

nomenclature, it would correctly stand in the order of " Spasmi," in the Nosology of Cullen, following simple diarrhœa; and the most correct name would be Malignant or Spasmodic Epidemic Diarrhœa. I therefore name it accordingly

## MALIGNANT EPIDEMIC DIARRHŒA.

It is an epidemic disease, neither contagious nor infectious, having in the progress of its symptoms two stages.*

### CHARACTER OF THE FIRST STAGE.

A sensation of general weakness over the whole body; languid pulse; sickness and pain about the stomach; purging and twitchings of the bowels; clammy feeling in the mouth; and a desire to drink more than usual.

---

* Infectious as well as non-infectious diseases may be epidemic.

### CHARACTER OF THE SECOND STAGE.

Extreme prostration of strength; incessant vomiting and purging of limpid fluid; total suppression of urine; intolerable thirst; cold breath, and general coldness of the body; sunken eyes; a dark blue aud corrugated appearance of the skin of the hands and feet, with violent spasms of the extremities and the bowels. In children,—vomiting; purging; great thirst; suppression of urine, and a general restlessness.

---

# CAUSES.

### REMOTE.

Not known, but presumed to arise from a peculiar constitution of atmosphere.

### PREDISPOSING.

Exposure to sudden changes of atmosphere; severe mental affliction; excessive fatigue; drunkenness; dyspepsia; in fact, every circumstance that tends to derange the system or diminish vital energy.

## EXCITING.

Anything that irritates the stomach or relaxes the bowels.

## PROXIMATE.

Violent purging and vomiting.

## PROGNOSIS.

Favourable in the first stage. { A diminution of purging and sickness; free secretion of urine; and coloured evacuations; a free pulse.

Favourable in the second stage. { Restoration of the pulse; warm breath; the vomiting and purging of a bilious character; a secretion of urine; and the colour of the extremities changing from blue to red.

## TREATMENT.

Indications $\left\{\begin{array}{l}\text{To invigorate the functions}\\ \text{of the liver, and suppress}\\ \text{the morbid evacuations.}\end{array}\right.$
in the
first stage.

### REMEDIES.

For children up to four years old :

> Calomel, five grains.
> Ginger, five grains.—Mix.

This powder to be given immediately, mixed in a little treacle, and two hours after the powder give the purgative draught :

> Powdered Rhubarb, ten grains.
> Castor Oil, half an ounce.—Mix.

From the age of four years to fourteen :

The powder ... $\left\{\begin{array}{l}\text{Calomel, six grains.}\\ \text{Ginger, six grains.—Mix.}\end{array}\right.$

The draught $\left\{\begin{array}{l}\text{Castor Oil, three-quarters of an ounce.}\\ \text{Tincture of Rhubarb, two drachms.}\\ \text{Powdered Rhubarb, eight grains.—Mix.}\end{array}\right.$

# From the age of fourteen and upwards:

The powder ... $\begin{cases} \text{Calomel, ten grains to fifteen.} \\ \text{Ginger, ten grains to twenty.—Mix.} \end{cases}$

The draught ... $\begin{cases} \text{Castor Oil and} \\ \text{Tincture of Rhubarb,} \\ \qquad \text{of each one ounce.—Mix.} \end{cases}$

During the progress of this stage, small doses of simple saline mixture or soda-water should be taken every half-hour.

Indications in the second stage. $\begin{cases} \text{To free the stomach and} \\ \text{bowels from their morbific} \\ \text{contents; to increase the} \\ \text{volume of blood, and} \\ \text{restore the circulation.} \end{cases}$

REMEDIES.

For children up to the age of four years:

Common Salt, one scruple.
Bicarbonate of Soda, six grains.
Chlorate of Potash, two grains.—Mix.
(For one dose.)

From four to fourteen years of age :

> Common Salt, one drachm.
> Bicarbonate of soda, ten grains.
> Chlorate of Potash, three grains.—Mix.

For persons above the age of fourteen years :

> Common Salt, two drachms.
> Bicarbonate of Soda, one scruple.
> Chlorate of Potash, seven grains.—Mix.

The above powders, dissolved in a small quantity of cold water, to be given every quarter of an hour until the excess of purging subsides, and the pulse is clearly perceptible : from which time extend the period between each dose, first to half an hour, then to one hour, and so on till both pulse and breathing are vigorous.  During the progress of this treatment, as much cold water may be taken as the patient desires ; the more the better.

The cramps are greatly relieved by a hot salt-water bath ; from seven to four-

teen pounds of common salt dissolved in a
sufficient quantity of water to cover the
whole body, and the patient to remain
in from ten to twenty minutes, at a degree
of heat from 110° to 120°; if the cramps
continue, the bath must be repeated every
two hours. The patient must be kept in
bed between blankets, with bottles of hot
water to the feet and legs; a free current
of fresh air should be allowed to pass
through the apartment, and, if possible,
directly over the face of the patient, the
body being kept as warm as possible. To
render the atmosphere of the room as
healthy as possible, curtains, carpets, and
all moveable furniture should be taken
away.

Solution for the injection :—

> Common Salt, three drachms.
> Bicarbonate of Soda, half a drachm.
> Chlorate of Potash, fifteen grains.
> Water, forty-eight ounces.—Mix.

To be slowly injected into the veins, at

E

a temperature of 100°; from sixteen to thirty-two ounces will be generally found sufficient to restore circulation in patients under fourteen years of age ; beyond this age, from forty-eight to eighty ounces may be injected, and repeated on the circulation again declining.

## DIRECTIONS FOR USING THE SALINE INJECTION.

Take especial care to have a good syringe, which must be free from oil and kept perfectly clean ; otherwise the saline matter will corrode the metal and render it unfit for the purpose. The syringe I have hitherto used, is a common enema syringe, having a fine silver canula about two inches long, slightly curved, and adapted to the elastic tube ; it is better to have the canula of this length, as it can be more readily commanded ; the aperture should be sloped on the side of the extremity, leaving the point rounded, otherwise some difficulty would be experienced in its introduction into the vein; the canula must be passed at least one inch within the vein. Any of the superficial veins may be selected; I have generally chosen the media on the upper extremity, or the saphena in the lower extremity. It is better to make an incision about an inch and a half long through the integuments, at the distance of half an inch from the vein, but parallel with it; draw the skin aside and cut through the cellular tissue, so as fully to expose the vein, under which pass a probe; raise the vein above the surface, and with the point of a lancet make a small longitudinal incision, into which the canula adapted to the elastic tube, being filled with the solution, must be introduced; it is better to let the probe remain until the desired quantity of solution be thrown in, for by taking it away the vein would bleed and become troublesome;

when done, return the vein to its place,
the integument will cover and protect it
from injury; draw the skin together by
adhesive plaster and bandage up the arm
after the usual manner. If required to
repeat the operation the same vein and
aperture will do, even for three or four
times; I have never seen inflammation
extend up the vein, nor any evil whatever
arise from the operation. The saline
solution should be made in a white wash-
hand basin, so that the sediment, if any,
may be seen and avoided. When about
thirty ounces of the fluid have been injected the patient will experience a general
uneasiness and tightness about the chest;
you have only to suspend the operation
for a few minutes, that the circulation may
equalize itself, afterwards progress slowly
till the pulse is fully restored; in general
a severe rigour will supervene, and last
from fifteen to twenty minutes, which will
be succeeded, in favourable cases, by a
corresponding reaction; the patient must

not be left by the surgeon for more than
two hours at a time.

When the vomiting, purging, and cramps
have subsided, and the pulse and warmth
of the body are restored, the patient may
be allowed to take broth, beef-tea, gruel,
and coffee, for the first forty-eight hours;
afterwards, rice and batter puddings, with
a gradual improvement in diet, till perfectly restored; spirits or wine should be
strictly avoided, but good malt liquor in
small draughts may be taken with advan-
tage.

Brandy, opium, and all such stimulants
are most injurious; nearly every person
that died in the Free Hospital had taken
one or all of these remedies previously to
their admission.

# CASES

## RESTORED BY THE SALINE INJECTION.

JOHN SCOTT MAYNE, aged thirteen, of Farringdon Street, seized with vomiting and purging at nine o'clock A.M., August 24, 1833. At nine P.M., found him in the extreme of collapse; requested that he might be immediately conveyed to the hospital; ordered a saline powder to be given every fifteen minutes, cold water *ad libitum*, and a hot saline bath. At half-past ten o'clock, the boy quite insensible, and at the point of dissolution; about thirty-two ounces of saline fluid were injected: before the operation was over, the clock in the hospital struck eleven; when, to the astonishment of all around, the boy asked, " What o'clock is it? "

"Ten," replied one of the nurses. "No," said the boy hastily, "it is eleven, for I counted it." The pulse returned; respiration free; the countenance resumed a healthy aspect, and animation pervaded the whole frame. The boy continued gradually to gain strength, and after eight days left the hospital, quite restored. This boy enjoyed excellent health afterwards, and is now a strong man.

J. MONUMENT, aged thirty-nine, residing at 194, Upper Thames Street,* a bricklayer. This man's habits were peculiarly temperate, having lived chiefly on vegetable diet, being a member of a society who object to eat animal food; he had long suffered from indigestion, and was of weakly constitution. First saw him at twelve o'clock at night, August 24th. He had suffered from the usual symptoms

---

* This man died in the spring of the year 1865, at the age of 71 years.

for two days; had been treated with opium and carminatives, from the first attack. Found him, as in the other case, advanced far in collapse; ordered a saline powder every fifteen minutes; a hot saline bath, and water *ad libitum*. Nine o'clock on the following morning, vitality only just perceptible; injected to the extent of forty-eight ounces; the pulse restored, and animation once more manifest throughout the frame. In this case, the diarrhœa continued, and after four hours the patient sunk almost to the point of death; he was again injected to the like extent, when again vitality dawned: the diarrhœa still continued, and he sunk a third time. A third injection was given to the extent of sixty-four ounces, and astringents of bark and opium were administered, when a third and lasting reanimation took place. From this time the patient gradually improved; and on being induced to live on animal food, and altogether on a more generous diet, he has been in better health than for several years previous to the attack.

MARGARET HARRIS, aged thirty-one years, had a family of five children, was admitted August 12th, 1833, from Johnson's Court, Fleet Street. The saline powders, and water *ad libitum*, were taken until one o'clock A.M., of the 13th, when twenty-four ounces of saline solution were injected, and an astringent mixture, consisting of tincture of opium and bark, was taken in small doses. From this time she gradually improved, and was discharged quite well, on the 22nd. Up to the present period her health continues good.

BRIAN SULLIVAN, aged thirty years, from No. 7, Richbell Place, admitted August 21st, 1833. He took the saline powders, and was twice injected to the extent of forty ounces each time. An astringent mixture, as in the above case, was taken after the second injection : he was discharged quite well on the 29th.—This patient had been left for dead after the first injection, and was absolutely measured for his coffin. He has enjoyed excellent health ever since.

Four other cases, the names and addresses of which are not correctly known, were restored by injection, in the year 1832.

Fifteen patients were restored from the collapsed stage of the disorder by injection, who all afterwards died from the effects of the consecutive fever, at periods varying from four to twenty-one days.

Much is yet to be learnt in the treatment and management of injected patients.

During the months of June and July, 1832, many patients were treated by large doses of common salt only ; and the two following cases are given to show that this plan of treatment (published in the *Lancet,* on the 9th of August, 1834, by

Mr. Beaman) was by no means new : it certainly arrested the progress of the malady, but all the patients so treated, died ; yet, the plan approaches nearer to the principle advanced by me, than any other : indeed it is only a modification of the same remedy.

PHILIP CLARK, aged twenty-seven years, by trade a chemist and druggist, from Lincoln, was admitted July 4th, 1832, at ten o'clock A.M. One ounce of salt, dissolved in half a pint of water, was given, every hour, till four o'clock P.M. on the following day, when he expired.

GEORGE HILL, aged fifty-three years, from No. 14, Fleur-de-lis Court, Fleet Street, admitted at eleven o'clock, A.M. July 6th, 1832. Treated after the like manner—died at seven o'clock P.M., the same day. All the patients treated after this mode had the hot saline bath.

*The following is a List of Patients who were admitted into the Free Hospital, during the years 1832 and 1833, whose names, ages, and residences are known; many others were restored, but, not knowing their places of abode, are omitted. These patients were all in the second or collapsed stage, and many of them had been treated and abandoned as lost by their medical attendants previously to their admission. They were all put under the saline remedies as laid down in the preceding part of this paper.*

| Date of admission. | Name. | Age. | Residence. | Date of discharge. |
|---|---|---|---|---|
| 1832. May 25 | Elizabeth Shay .. | 37 | 12, Blue-court, Saffron-hill.... | June 14 |
| | Julia Brushney .. | 9 | Ditto .... | 10 |
| | Ellen Brushney .. | 30 | Ditto .... | 10 |
| June 1 | Mary Samford.... | 55 | Ditto .... | 8 |
| 2 | Catherine Ross .. | 28 | 11, Ditto .... | 12 |
| 3 | Mary Higgins .. | 19 | Onslow-street, Saffron-hill.... | 8 |
| 10 | Flora McCormack. | 51 | Nurse at the Hospital ........ | 18 |
| July 7 | John Day .... .. | 49 | 5, Lilley-street, Saffron-hill .. | July 10 |
| 10 | William Taylor .. | 26 | 9, Field-lane.................. | 10 |
| 11 | Francis Feathers.. | 35 | 37, Dillon-street.............. | 16 |
| 12 | Margaret Lane .. | 2 | 3, Caroline-court, Saffron-hill . | 13 |
| 14 | Lawrence Denning | 35 | 1, George-alley, Field-lane.... | 28 |
| 15 | Margaret Newman | 7 | 6, Field-lane.............. | 18 |
| | Margaret Farrel .. | 11 | 5, Field-lane............ | 20 |
| | Michael Niven.... | 1 | Ditto .................. | 30 |
| 16 | George Mackie .. | 29 | 38, Fleet-lane ................ | 20 |
| | William Bonam .. | 35 | 8, George-alley, Field-lane .... | 25 |
| | William Moor .... | 1 | 6, George-alley .............. | 21 |
| 17 | Richard Gregory.. | 35 | West-street .................. | Aug. 6 |
| | Jane Davies ...... | 30 | 21, Fleet-lane ................ | June 25 |
| 18 | William Roberts.. | 60 | Clark's-buildings, St. Bride's.. | Aug. 1 |
| | Ann Clayton...... | 35 | Black-bear-alley............. | June 22 |
| 19 | James Dillon .... | 37 | 24, Red-lion-court, Saffron-hill | 23 |
| 20 | Mary Field ...... | 52 | 8, Red-lion-court ........... | Aug. 9 |
| 21 | Margaret Mahoney | 32 | New-court, Saffron-hill ...... | July 23 |
| | Elizabeth Tower.. | 32 | 3, New-court ................ | 24 |
| 22 | Catherine Hughes | 30 | St. Sepulchre's Workhouse .. | 25 |
| | Hannah Reading.. | 6 | 2, Greyhound-court .......... | 25 |
| 23 | William Spencer.. | 57 | Bull's-head-court, Smithfield.. | 24 |
| | William Clifford .. | 4 | Saffron-hill ................. | 25 |

| Date of admission. | Name. | Age. | Residence. | Date of discharge. |
|---|---|---|---|---|
| 1832. | | | | |
| July 24 | Mary Wayte...... | 43 | 4, Portpool-lane.............. | July 27 |
| 26 | John Rolland .... | 12 | Duke of York's School........ | 31 |
| 29 | William Jackson | 36 | Workhouse, St. Mary-le-Strand | Aug. 3 |
| | John Harrison ... | 40 | 3, Caroline-place, Saffron-hill.. | 11 |
| 30 | Mary Cook ...... | 21 | Gray's-inn Workhouse........ | 22 |
| Aug. 1 | Mary Bough .... | 35 | Ditto        ........ | 22 |
| 2 | Peter Pedley...... | 48 | Ditto        ........ | 9 |
| 5 | Martha Mastey .. | 10 | 16, Little Ormond-yard ...... | 14 |
| 7 | George Mills .,.. | 24 | 3, Fox-court, Saffron-hill...... | 11 |
| 9 | Stephen Dyer ..,.. | 14 | 2, Saffron-hill................ | 13 |
| 11 | John Smith ...... | 23 | St. Sepulchre's Workhouse.... | 27 |
| 14 | Ellen Power...... | 37 | 2, Union-court .............. | 23 |
| 18 | Marian Isle ...... | 20 | St. Paul's, Covent-garden .... | 30 |
| | Jane Dallastone .. | 21 | 110, Great Saffron-hill ........ | 27 |
| | Rebecca Villiers .. | 48 | 8, Plough-court .............. | 27 |
| | Elizabeth Wilson.. | 64 | 30, Rutland-court ............ | 27 |
| 20 | Peter Adams...... | 64 | 14, Glass-house-yard.......... | 27 |
| | Robert Carter .... | 43 | St. Sepulchre's Workhouse.... | 27 |
| | Thomas Smith.... | 64 | St. Mary-le-Strand............ | Sept. 1 |
| 22 | Sarah Mercroft .. | 55 | Church-court ................ | Aug. 30 |
| 23 | Mary Scott ...... | 52 | 20, Fetter-lane .............. | Sept. 3 |
| 25 | Caroline Connor.. | 20 | 8, Caroline-court ............ | Aug. 30 |
| | James Parry...... | 33 | St. Mary-le-Strand .......... | 30 |
| 26 | James Merchant.. | 35 | 6, Plough-court .............. | 30 |
| 28 | Marian Bougard.. | 2½ | St. Sepulchre's Workhouse.... | 31 |
| 31 | Ann Haycroft .... | 6 | Gray's-inn Workhouse........ | Sept. 4 |
| Sept. 5 | Henry Stamford.. | 69 | 28, Brook-street.............. | 7 |
| | Elizabeth Smith.. | 38 | 14, Portpool-lane ............ | 10 |
| 7 | James Ward...... | 25 | Drury-court, Drury-lane...... | 27 |
| 12 | Mrs. Smedley .... | 56 | 54, Saffron-hill .............. | 21 |
| | Jane Briant ...... | 41 | 49, Saffron-hill .............. | 18 |
| | James Sopaci .. .. | 41 | 6, Nevil's-court, Fetter-lane .. | 18 |
| 13 | Sarah Richards .. | 21 | 7, Saffron-hill ................ | 21 |
| | James Davis...... | 16 | Glass-house-yard ............ | 25 |
| | Mary Davis...... | 48 | Ditto        ........ | Oct. 1 |
| 21 | Henry Allen...... | 77 | Dean's-court, Old Bailey...... | Sept.23 |
| | John Eleneugh .. | 27 | 9, Eyre-street-hill ............ | Oct. 1 |
| 30 | Patrick Flinn .... | 14 | Saffron-hill ................ | 17 |
| Oct. 11 | Sarah Jones...... | 13 | Baldwin's-gardens .......... | 22 |
| 12 | Ann Smith ...... | 62 | Bear-lane.................... | 19 |
| 1833. | | | | |
| Aug. 10 | George Nicholls .. | 40 | 32, Portpool-lane ............ | Aug.21 |
| 12 | Margaret Harris.. | 31 | Johnson's-court............. | 22 |
| 18 | Charles Watt .... | 27 | 28, Greenhill's-rents ........ | 26 |
| 19 | Robert Lucas .... | 23 | Leadenhall-street ............ | 22 |
| 21 | Sarah Walker .... | 46 | 85, Theobald's-road .......... | 28 |
| | Brian Sullivan.... | 30 | 7, Richbell-place ............ | 29 |
| Sept.15 | William Wilson .. | 50 | 6, Black-bear-alley .......... | Sept.21 |

*The following Statement is from the Lancet of February
2nd, 1833.—The Prescriptions being the same as
inserted in the directions for Treatment, are omitted.*

## MALIGNANT CHOLERA.

AT THE HOSPITAL IN GREVILLE STREET, HOLBORN.

(*Communicated by the Central Board.*)

Guildhall, December 18th, 1832.

Sir,—I have this morning received a communication from Mr. Marsden, and transmit the same for the information of the Central Board of Health.

I have the honour to be, Sir,

Your most obedient Servant,

J. F. De Grave,

To W. Maclean, Esq.      Hon. Med. Sec.

2, Thavies Inn, December 15th, 1832.

Dear Sir,—In conformity with your request of the 6th instant, and for the information of the "Central Board," I beg to lay before you the following statement of the number of patients admitted into the Free Hospital, Greville Street, up to the 12th of October last, with the modes of treatment and the results.

One hundred and eighty-four patients afflicted with Malignant Cholera, in the second stage—that is, having no pulsation of the wrist, livid extremities, &c. &c.

Of this number seventeen died, either on their way to the Hospital, or immediately after their admission, no medicine having been administered.

Eighteen were treated by various plans, previously to the introduction of saline remedies, of whom thirteen died, and five recovered.

Thirteen who were treated by the above plans, were, after all hope of recovery was lost, injected with saline solution, at the temperature of one hundred and ten degrees. Eleven died and two recovered.

Twenty-three were treated in the first instance by calomel and opium, brandy, ammonia, external stimulants, &c., without success; afterwards by the saline medicine. Eighteen died and five recovered.

Of twenty-eight who had taken freely of opium and brandy previously to their admission, but were afterwards put on the saline treatment, twenty-one died, and seven recovered. Of four, who were aged and previously diseased, treated by saline remedies only, all died. Of eighty-one who were treated by the saline remedies alone, seven died and seventy-four recovered.

In addition to the above number, three hundred and fifteen patients (who were not reported), labouring under the first stage of the complaint, were treated by calomel and vegetable purgatives; twelve cases ran into the second stage, and were treated by the saline remedies; eventually four died; all the rest recovered.—I am, dear Sir, your obedient servant,

W. MARSDEN.

## MALIGNANT CHOLERA IN LONDON.

*Comparative View of the various Modes of Treatment adopted in Cholera, within the jurisdiction of the City of London Board of Health, transmitted by* MR. J. F. DE GRAVE.

|  | Cases. | Deaths. | Recoveries. | Deaths percent. | Recoveries percent. |
|---|---|---|---|---|---|
| Calomel and Opium ........ | 196 | 112 | 84 | 57·14 | 42·86 |
| Opium .................... | 81 | 47 | 34 | 58· | 42· |
| Calomel.................... | 75 | 35 | 40 | 46·66 | 53·34 |
| Stimulants ............... | 63 | 42 | 21 | 66·66 | 33·33 |
| Combination of Salts proposed by Dr. Stevens .. . | 25 | 22 | 3 | 88· | 12· |
| Combination of Salts used at the Free Hospital ...... | 26 | 8 | 18 | 30·77 | 69 32 |
| Venous injection, in ditto .. | 20 | 18 | 2 | 0· | 10· |
| Miscellaneous............. | 17 | 8 | 9 | 47·06 | 52·94 |

## PRECAUTIONARY MEASURES.

IN order to preserve the healthy from an attack of this disease, the following plan of diet and medicine should be pursued. Animal and vegetable food, well cooked, may be taken once or twice a day; fish, if quite fresh, is not objectionable; and to persons who do not take wine daily, malt liquor in moderate quan-

F

tity, is in general the best beverage : wine-drinkers should not exceed from four to six glasses of the best Port, and that ought not to be taken sooner than one hour and a half after dinner; tea or coffee taken early after dinner, is at all times bad; and spirit-and-water, or any other fluid in large quantity, is also injurious. Small doses of calomel and rhubarb, about three grains of the former to ten of the latter, should be taken about once a month; and persons troubled with indigestion would be benefited by taking twice a day, between meals, the following stomachic powder, mixed in about three or four table spoonfuls of cold water.

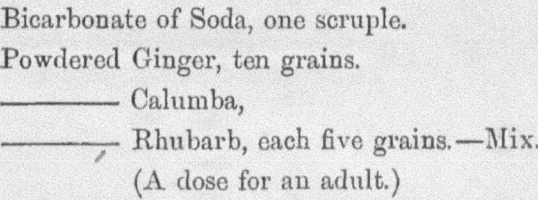

Bicarbonate of Soda, one scruple.
Powdered Ginger, ten grains.
———— Calumba,
———— Rhubarb, each five grains.—Mix.
(A dose for an adult.)

Ripe fruits may be taken in moderation without the slightest mischief. I believe all kinds of shell-fish during the autumnal season to be decidedly objectionable; but less so if cooked.

Sudden changes of temperature, and all circumstances that weaken the constitutional powers, either in diet or in *habits*, must be carefully avoided; as they have a great tendency to predispose all persons to the immediate influence of the specific disease.

In publishing another Edition of this Treatise, I must here beg to remark that, during the prevalence of the last visitation of this epidemic, upwards of 3,000 patients admitted at the Royal Free Hospital were treated with success on the principle here laid down.

## The following Testimonials were presented to the Author in the Year 1833.

At a Meeting of the Board of Health for the City of London, held at the Guildhall of the said City, on Friday, the 15th day of February, 1833—

RESOLVED UNANIMOUSLY—

That the thanks of this Board be given to the Medical Officers of the Local Boards of Health within this City, for their very prompt, able, and efficient co-operation during the late prevalence of the Spasmodic Cholera ; and for their zealous and benevolent attendance on the poor and destitute, who were attacked with that pestilential disease in their respective districts.

The Board feel highly gratified at the devotion and liberality with which these Gentlemen accepted the troublesome and responsible appointment, without the consideration of fee or reward ; and has now the additional satisfaction to acknowledge the honourable zeal and perseverance with which the arduous and anxious duties were performed.

(Signed)

By order of the Board,

CHARLES PEARSON, *Chairman.*

I. F. DE GRAVE, *Hon. Med. Sec.*

To WILLIAM MARSDEN, ESQ., *Surgeon.*

At the fifth Annual General Meeting of the Governors of the Free Hospital, Greville Street, Hatton Garden, for the cure of Malignant Diseases, held February 28th, 1833, at the Board Room of the Institution—

ALDERMAN HARMER *in the Chair,*

IT WAS UNANIMOUSLY RESOLVED—

That the grateful thanks of the Meeting be given to Mr. WILLIAM MARSDEN, Surgeon of this Institution, for his zealous, indefatigable, and successful exertions in the discharge of his professional duties, during the prevalence of the late Epidemic Disease, called Spasmodic Cholera ; and also for his unremitting and humane attention to, and successful treatment of, the diseased and destitute persons who have applied to this Hospital for medical relief, whereby many thousand individuals who would otherwise have been pining in wretchedness and misery, a burthen to themselves and a pest to society, have been restored to health and comfort.

That the above Resolution be fairly transcribed and presented to Mr. MARSDEN, and that it also be inserted in the six following Papers, viz. :—*The Times, Morning Herald, Morning Chronicle, Morning Post, Courier,* and *Dispatch.*

C. N. HUNT, *Hon. Sec.*

WYMAN AND SONS, PRINTERS, GREAT QUEEN STREET, LONDON, W.C.

*With Coloured Plates from Life, Illustrative Cases and Formulæ.*
*8vo., cloth, price 6s. 6d.*

# A NEW AND SUCCESSFUL MODE

OF TREATING

# CERTAIN FORMS OF CANCER.

To which is prefixed a Practical and Systematic Description of all the Varieties of this Disease, showing how to distinguish them one from another, and from Tumours, &c., simulating them.

## By ALEXANDER MARSDEN, M.D., F.R.C.S.E.

*Surgeon to the Cancer Hospital, London and Brompton, and to the Royal Free Hospital, Gray's Inn Road, late Surgeon to the Ambulance before Sevastopol, &c. &c.*

## PREFACE.

THE plan of treatment recommended in this volume has been successful in my own hands, and in those of many other surgeons who have adopted it. It is not intended to supersede the use of the knife, but to be used for those cases in which that instrument would be useless, or in which a good caustic can do the work better; as such I offer it to the profession at large.

In the First Part I have endeavoured to give a *concise* but *systematic* description of every form of Cancer and Tumour simulating Cancer, in order that practitioners and students, whose opportunities of studying this disease have been limited, may be enabled at once to distinguish each variety by its own peculiarities. I am not aware that *this* has before been attempted, and must plead it as my excuse for the many shortcomings of the present volume.

It affords me great pleasure to acknowledge the valuable services Mr. Hayward, our excellent house surgeon at the Cancer Hospital, has always rendered me in all my investigations; and to our artist, Mr. C. D'Alton, I feel deeply indebted for the beautiful and unique collection of drawings from life his pencil has produced.

65, LINCOLN'S-INN FIELDS, LONDON.

## CONTENTS.

"This disease has always baffled the skill of the medical profession more than any other; but since the establishment of the Cancer Hospital in 1851, by the father of the author of this work, upwards of 8,000 cases have been collected, and a field of observation formed, such as cannot be found elsewhere. The immense experience of Dr. Marsden on this subject entitles his work to a most careful perusal by all interested in the subject. The first part is written in a very clear and terse style, and thoroughly carries out the promise of the title-page. The second treats in the same clear and straightforward manner of a particular and successful mode of treatment, which has now stood the test of 12 years' trial. The book is illustrated with coloured plates, and the details of the treatment of 15 cases."—*London Mirror.*

LONDON : JOHN CHURCHILL & SONS, NEW BURLINGTON STREET.